Fashion Fairy Princess

With fairy big thanks to Sally Morgan

First published in the UK in 2014 by Scholastic Children's Books
An imprint of Scholastic Ltd
Euston House, 24 Eversholt Street
London, NW1 1DB, UK
Registered office: Westfield Road, Southam, Warwickshire, CV47 0RA
SCHOLASTIC and associated logos are trademarks and/or registered
trademarks of Scholastic Inc.

Text copyright © Scholastic Ltd, 2014
Cover copyright © Pixie Potts, Beehive Illustration Agency, 2014
Inside illustration copyright © David Shephard, The Bright Agency, 2014

The right of Poppy Collins to be identified as the author
of this work has been asserted by her.

ISBN 978 1407 13955 5

A CIP catalogue record for this book is available from the British Library.

Printed and bound by CPI Group (UK) Ltd, Croydon, CR0 4YY
Papers used by Scholastic Children's Books are made
from wood grown in sustainable forests.

1 3 5 7 9 10 8 6 4 2

www.scholastic.co.uk
www.fashionfairyprincess.com

Fashion Fairy Princess

Buttercup

in Glitter Ocean

POPPY COLLINS

SCHOLASTIC

Dream
Mountain

Jewel Forest

Sparkle
City

Star
Valley

River
Sapphire

Shimmer Island

Glitter Ocean

Welcome to the world of the fashion fairy princesses! Join Buttercup and friends on their magical adventures in fairyland.

They can't wait to visit

Glitter Ocean!

Can you?

Chapter 1

"Please could you pass me the petal pancakes, Buttercup?" asked Violet, eyeing the tall stack of fluffy pink cakes hungrily. "They look delicious."

"They are," said Bluebell, pouring rose-coloured syrup on to her second helping. "I think they might be the nicest I've ever tasted."

Buttercup passed the silver plate of

pancakes to her friend. It was a sunny Saturday morning and the fashion fairy princesses – Violet, Rosa, Buttercup and Bluebell – were having breakfast on the jewelled patio of Glimmershine Palace. All around them the glittering pink and purple flowers of the palace's gardens fluttered in the gentle breeze.

"It's such a beautiful day," said Buttercup, taking a sip of nectar from the flower-shaped glass in front of her. "I can't wait to get down to the palace stables."

"Oh look," said Violet, "here's Ferdinand with the fairy-mail. I wonder if he has anything exciting for me."

Ferdinand was a beautiful metallic blue firefly and a fairy-flyer. The fairy-flyers picked up and delivered the fashion fairy princesses' fairy-mail from all over Sparkle City.

Violet looked a little disappointed as Ferdinand buzzed quickly past her chair. He also passed Rosa and Bluebell but landed gently next to a surprised Buttercup.

"I wasn't expecting anything," said Buttercup excitedly as she thanked Ferdinand and reached into his saddlebag.

When she pulled out her hand, she was holding a large gold glittering shell.

"What a beautiful shell," said Bluebell.

"It looks like it came from Glitter Ocean," said Rosa, peering closer. "Do you know someone from Glitter Ocean, Buttercup?"

"Only my Great-aunt Melinda. She's a mermaid and lives near Coral Castle with the other merpeople," answered Buttercup, examining the shell carefully, "but I haven't heard from her since last year's Annual Fairy Festival."

"Aren't you going to open it?" said Violet, desperate to know what was inside. "Perhaps it's a present."

Buttercup looked at the large, flat shell in her hand and tried to open it with her delicate fingers, but nothing happened.

"Let me have a go," said Violet, reaching for the shell.

"Violet, it's Buttercup's invitation. Let her open it," said Rosa gently. "Buttercup, why don't you try using a little fairy-dust? Perhaps it was closed with fairy magic."

"Good idea, Rosa," said Violet. "Sorry, Buttercup, I was only trying to help."

Buttercup took out a small pouch of fairy-dust from the skirt of her dress and sprinkled a little over the shell. With a puff of golden glitter, the shell opened to reveal a shining yellow invitation. Buttercup read it out in her gentle voice.

" 'Fashion Fairy Princess Buttercup and friends are most cordially invited to King Neptune's Annual Glitter Ball to be held at Coral Castle on Saturday the. . .' Oh my goodness," said Buttercup, "it says  it's tonight! Dress code: ocean fabulous."

"Tonight?" said Bluebell. "That doesn't give us much time. Where in fairyland will we find something ocean fabulous at this short notice?"

"Wait, there's something written on the back," said Rosa. "Turn it over, Buttercup, and read it out."

Buttercup turned over the pretty yellow invitation, and sure enough there was a note from Great-aunt Melinda written on the back.

Dearest Buttercup,

The Glitter Ball is always such fun, so naturally I wanted to invite my favourite niece. I'm sure you fashion fairy princesses have hundreds of gorgeous gowns to choose from, but just in case you aren't sure of what to wear, I have reserved four dresses for you at Serena Seaspray's Ocean Emporium in the Sparkle City Mall.

Looking forward to seeing you,

Hugs and sparkles,

Great-aunt Melinda xxx

"Let's head to the mall right away," said Rosa excitedly. "If we go now, we should have enough time."

"I don't know," Buttercup frowned. "I did say I would groom the palace ponies this morning."

"Come on, Buttercup," said Violet, hopping off her chair and gently tugging Buttercup out of hers. "How often do we get invited to Glitter Ocean? Think of all of the beautiful sea creatures we'll see on the way."

"All right, then," said Buttercup, brightening. "A Glitter Ball will be a lot of fun."

"Of course it will," said Violet, clapping her hands. "It'll be an adventure."

And with that the four princesses fluttered their wings and flew off to the Sparkle City Mall.

Chapter 2

Rosa, Buttercup, Violet and Bluebell
landed softly outside the Sparkle City
Mall and flew over to the enchanted
map in the shining crystal entrance
hall. It was Saturday morning and all
the shops were full of bustling fashion
fairies in fantastic outfits. Usually, the
four friends liked nothing more than to
wander around, looking at all the fabulous

window displays, but today they were on an important mission: Operation Ocean Fabulous.

"I think Serena Seaspray's Ocean Emporium is on the third floor," said Rosa, looking at the map. "Let's fly up there as quickly as we can. It's so busy in here today."

The princesses fluttered quickly up to the third floor and stood together in front of a shop unlike any they had seen before. The outside was covered in hundreds of thousands of sparkling seashells, and the windows, instead of being made of normal glass, were made of giant crystal fish tanks filled with glittering water. Inside the tanks floated beautiful dresses in all different colours.

"Wow," said Buttercup, pointing at a gorgeous yellow silk dress that was gently

floating inside the tank in front of her. "I would love to wear something like that."

"Well, we won't get the chance if we don't get a move on," said Rosa, smiling. "Let's get inside and take a look."

The inside of the shop was just as impressive as the outside. The walls were decorated with even more seashells and there were ocean-themed displays everywhere they looked. Bluebell immediately rushed over to the nearest one, where necklaces were draped artistically on the branches of coral.

"Oh my goodness," she said, "a sapphire stingray pendant! And look, those blue spots are real sapphires! Aren't they beautiful?"

"Princesses, we have to focus," said Rosa, steering Bluebell away from the jewellery display. "Let's check out these dresses."

As she spoke, a pretty fairy wearing a bright dress that was covered in pearls and red coral beads glided over to them.

"Well, hello there," she said brightly. "My name is Serena Seaspray, and this is my shop. Are you looking for anything in particular?"

"Yes, please," said Buttercup, flushing

slightly and
searching
in her bag
for the
invitation.
"You see,
I have this
invitation
from my
Great-aunt
Melinda.
She said she
had reserved some dresses?"

"Of course!" said Serena Seaspray,
immediately folding Buttercup into a big
hug and then fluttering a few steps back,
just far enough to take a good look at
her. "You must be Fashion Fairy Princess
Buttercup! Darling Melinda sent me an
urgent fairy-mail this morning and told

me to look out for you. She's an old family friend, you know. So you are attending the Glitter Ball? You must be very excited."

Serena glanced across at Violet, Rosa and Bluebell. "Oh yes, the dresses she picked out for you will look wonderful. They really are ocean fabulous, if I do say so myself. I'll just go and get them. Feel free to browse while I'm gone. You might find some nice accessories to go with them." Serena disappeared into a back room and the fairy princesses immediately started exploring the shop.

"Oooh, look at these sandals," said Bluebell, slipping her tiny foot into a bright blue pair of flip-flops covered in shimmering crushed oyster shells. "Aren't they beautiful?"

"I love them," said Rosa, "and they

come in pink coral, too. I hope they have
them in my size. Buttercup, I think there's
a pair over there in a glittery sand colour.
You should definitely try them on."

But Buttercup couldn't hear her. She
was peering into a large jewellery display
cabinet. Inside, surrounded by shiny pebbles
and silvery fishing nets, were four glimmering
seahorse hair clips decorated with tiny shells.

Before she had the chance to point them out to her friends, Serena called them into the fitting room at the back of the shop.

"Now princesses, I do hope you like them," Serena said. "We don't have much time to make any adjustments."

She pulled back the shell-patterned curtain of the fitting room to reveal four of the most beautiful dresses they had ever seen.

The dresses had no straps and the bodices were covered in tiny glittering seashells and pearls. But this wasn't what the fairy princesses loved most about them. What they loved most of all were the skirts. These were made from paper-thin scales of delicate silk that fell in layer upon layer and then flared out at the knee to make the fairies' legs look just like mermaids' tails.

The fairy princesses carefully stepped

into the delicate dresses. They fitted like a dream, and even better than that, there was a dress in each of their favourite colours! Rosa's dress was a pale coral pink, Buttercup's a shimmering golden yellow, Violet's was a deep, rich purple and Bluebell's was an inky ocean blue.

"Oh my goodness," said Violet, looking at their reflections in the seashell-framed mirror. "We look like four mermaid princesses."

"You do look beautiful, but something's missing," said Serena Seaspray, frowning at the fairy princesses. "Let me see," she said, fluttering out of the changing room.

When Serena came back she was carrying the four beautiful seahorse hair clips that Buttercup had seen earlier. They were a little wet, but otherwise completed their outfits perfectly.

"There," said Serena proudly, "now you look ocean fabulous!" And when the four fairies looked at themselves in the mirror, they had to agree.

Then Bluebell showed Serena the pretty sandals she had found, and all four fairy princesses tried them on. They looked perfect with their outfits, so they handed over their bags of fairy-dust and bought them, along with the dresses and hair clips. The fashion fairy princesses thanked Serena for all her help.

Serena gave them a big hug. "It's a great honour to be of service to the fashion fairy princesses, and I am always happy to help an old friend. Give Melinda my love, won't you, Buttercup?"

Buttercup nodded, and the four princesses headed back to Glimmershine Palace to pack up the rest of their things and begin their journey to Glitter Ocean.

Chapter 3

The invitation had said that there would be a carriage waiting for them at Sunshine Bay, not far outside Sparkle City, and that the carriage would take them the rest of the way to Coral Castle, deep in the heart of Glitter Ocean.

"Tell me why we don't come here more often," said Violet, as she landed softly on the glittering white sandy beach

of Sunshine Bay. All around them, excited
fairies were hopping in and out of the
waves and playing fun beach games.

"I know," said Bluebell, landing just in time to catch a tiny beach ball that was hurtling towards them. "We always have a great time when we go to the beach. It's a shame we don't have more time to stay and play." She tossed the ball back gently.

"Let's promise to all come back again soon," Buttercup said, eyeing a group of fairies with buckets and nets heading off to some rock pools further around the bay.

"Look over there," said Rosa, distracted by something along the shore. "That must be our carriage. My goodness! It's incredible!"

The fairy princesses immediately looked over to where she was pointing, and there it was, the most magnificent carriage, waiting for them at the edge of the water. The carriage was made from a giant clamshell and decorated with tiny pink and silver shells. The shells were arranged in such a way that it looked like the carriage was a glittering pink wave crashing on to the shore. In the water in front of the carriage, the princesses could just make out the bobbing heads of two seahorses wearing tiny little crowns.

"Are those seahorses going to take us all the way to Coral Castle?" asked Buttercup, almost overcome with excitement.

"Let's go and find out!" said Rosa, smiling at her friend.

The fashion fairy princesses fluttered towards the carriage. When they got there, they were called over by one of the seahorses at the front of the carriage.

"Hello there. My name is Periwinkle and this is Follyfin," he said, nodding towards the seahorse next to him. "We are King Neptune's personal seahorses and we will be taking you to Coral Castle. Which one of you is Princess Buttercup?"

"I am," said Buttercup, her ears flushing with embarrassment. "I'm very pleased to meet you."

Periwinkle nodded and smiled. "I see you are wearing beach clothes. If you like, you could go for a swim while we wait for the other two seahorses to arrive."

"Hooray!" said Violet, putting her weekend bag into the carriage. "Nice to meet you, Periwinkle and Follyfin. Come on, princesses, let's have a swim."

She slipped off her purple sarong to reveal a glittering purple swimsuit with a lilac frill around the bottom. Then she kicked off her sandals and hopped into the water. Buttercup, Rosa and Bluebell weren't far behind. It was a hot day and the princesses had had a busy morning, so they were all glad to cool off and relax in the sparkling waves.

"I know," said Rosa, popping her head above the water, "why don't we get some fairy-frost ice cream? I'm sure I saw a stand when I arrived."

"Good idea," said Bluebell, who had been jumping over the tiny waves.

She and Rosa headed off up the beach to the ice-cream stand while Buttercup and Violet lay on the soft sand and dried their wings in the warm breeze.

They were dozing in the fairyland sunshine when they heard Periwinkle calling to them. "Princesses, I would like to introduce you to Puck and Starlight," he said, nodding towards two shiny blue seahorses, who were also wearing gold crowns.

"Pleased to meet you," said Violet, sitting up and dusting sand off her wings. "I like your crowns – they look really pretty."

"Thank you," said Starlight. "We wear them because we are the royal seahorses."

Buttercup smiled at the seahorses and at Violet. She loved how her friend always seemed so comfortable no matter who she was talking to. Buttercup was happy chatting to her friends and with animals, but she often felt shy around new people. She wondered what it would be like to be as brave and confident as Violet.

"Sorry to keep you waiting," said Bluebell, fluttering up the beach with Rosa. "There was a queue. Here you are, Buttercup." She handed her a delicious-looking swirly pink ice cream.

"Is it time to go?" asked Rosa, handing a chocolate ice cream to Violet.

"Yes," said Periwinkle, "as soon as you are ready."

The princesses quickly pulled on their sarongs and beach dresses and tied back their hair with their new hair clips. They would style it properly later when they got ready for the ball.

"What are we waiting for! Let's go," said Violet, taking a big slurp of her ice cream and jumping into the carriage. The other fairy princesses followed, falling on to the big soft cushions inside.

"It's not far to Coral Castle from here," said Periwinkle, who was attaching the other seahorses to the carriage with long strands of seaweed. "If the weather stays fine, we should be able to get you there in good time for the Glitter Ball."

"Thank you," said Buttercup excitedly as the seahorses started to pull the carriage forward.

As the carriage began to move further

from the shore, the princesses noticed that
the water was rising around them.

"Um, excuse me, Periwinkle," said
Violet, clearing her throat nervously, "but
we appear to be sinking."

"Please don't worry, princesses," laughed
Periwinkle. "The carriage will travel the
rest of the way under the water. It's much

faster this way. And don't be concerned about breathing. You have all been invited into Glitter Ocean by a mermaid, and so the ocean will welcome you and allow you to breathe underwater."

"Are you quite sure?" said Violet doubtfully as the water reached her chest.

"Absolutely," said Periwinkle, urging the other seahorses to dive deeper. "It is ocean magic. The merpeople take care of the ocean, and in return, the ocean promises to look after the merpeople and their guests."

Violet, Rosa, Buttercup and Bluebell weren't convinced, so each of them took a deep breath and shut their eyes as their heads slipped below the water's warm, shimmery surface. When they opened their eyes, they were surrounded by glittering bubbles and shoals of rainbow-coloured fish. Buttercup gasped, and instead of getting a mouthful of water, she found she could breathe just as she could on land.

"Isn't it beautiful?" she said, looking around her at all the colourful fishes.

"Buttercup!" said Bluebell excitedly. "You can talk underwater!"

"So can you!" giggled Buttercup.

"Oh yes!" said Bluebell.

The fairy princesses laughed and joked together as the carriage moved slowly through the warm silky water, taking it in turns to point out interesting fish and corals they spotted along the way.

"Look," said Buttercup, pointing at some multicoloured fluttering fish that were swimming alongside the carriage. "Aren't those called party fish?"

"They are party fish, yes," said Periwinkle from the front of the coach.

"If you listen carefully, you will be able to
hear the music they are dancing to. They
make it themselves. You will see lots of
party fish at the Glitter Ball. They are the
best dancers in Glitter Ocean."

The princesses danced about in their
seats to the music from the party fish.

They were having lots of fun, blowing bubbles to one another and waving at all the tiny fish, when all of a sudden a dark shadow fell over the carriage.

"It can't be," said Buttercup, peering out of the carriage. "They are so rare. I never thought I would see one."

"It can't be what?" asked Rosa, curious. "What is it, Buttercup?"

But Buttercup was staring up at the darkly glittering shadow above their heads.

Chapter 4

"It's a glimmer whale," said Periwinkle, looking up at the enormous sparkly purple whale swimming above their heads, "and you are right, Buttercup, they are very rare indeed. Please don't worry, fairy princesses," he continued, seeing their stunned expressions. "They may look scary, but they are gentlest creatures in all Glitter Ocean. You are very lucky to have seen one. I wonder what has brought it this way. I've never seen one around here before. Hang on tight, fairies – I'm taking us up to find out what's going on."

With that, Periwinkle and the other seahorses darted upwards and drew the carriage level with the purple whale's enormous eye.

"Are you sure he isn't dangerous?" asked Bluebell nervously. Now that the princesses were closer to the whale, they could see just how big he really was. He was about twenty times the length of their tiny carriage. His smooth skin was a glittering purple, with pearly white patches on his sides and stomach. Buttercup nodded. Even though the whale was so big, she could tell that he was a gentle creature. She wished she could swim out of the carriage and talk to the whale, but she was too shy.

The whale looked at Periwinkle and let out a low booming moan and a series of short clicks.

"Hmm, I'm afraid it isn't good news, fairy princesses," said Periwinkle. "The glimmer whale says that there is bad weather up ahead. The ride might be a little bumpy from now on."

The seahorses set off again towards Coral Castle and the glimmer whale gave one flick of his enormous tail and swam off into the blue ocean. The fairy princesses settled back down and looked out of the carriage as they passed through some of the pretty sea villages in Glitter Ocean.

"Look," said Rosa, pointing towards a clamshell cottage with a little coral fence, "the merpeople have made their houses out of shells. They're so pretty."

Buttercup admired the lovely little cottages but then glanced nervously ahead. She was starting to get worried about the weather. She could feel that the ocean current was getting much stronger, making her long, wispy blonde hair swirl around her. The carriage had been moving more and more slowly and she had noticed that nearly all the fish they had seen had been swimming in the opposite direction to them.

"Buttercup! Did you see those pink starfish on the rock we just passed?" said Violet. "There they were, standing all tall and proud, and then they disappeared into the rock as soon as we went by. Do you know what they're called?"

"Erm . . . sorry, no, I missed them," said Buttercup, distracted by a cloud of glitter in the water around them. "It sounds like they were a kind of dazzle star."

"Are you OK, Buttercup?" asked Bluebell, concerned that her friend had been very quiet for a while now. "Are you feeling seasick?"

"I'm fine," said Buttercup, giving a small smile, "but can you see all that glitter in the water?"

"Yes," said Bluebell, "I just got a little bit in my eye. It's very pretty, though. What do you think it is?"

"I'm not sure," said Buttercup, "but I think we might be heading into a glitter storm."

"What's a glitter storm?" said Rosa, frowning.

"A glitter storm is when the current in the ocean gets so strong that it scoops up all the glittery sand on the ocean floor and sends it flying around like hailstones," explained Buttercup. "We've been moving slowly for some time. My guess is it's because the current is too strong for the seahorses. They must be getting tired."

Just as she finished, the carriage gave a sharp jerk sideways. The princesses held on to their seats, scared that it was going to tip over.

Chapter 5

"Don't worry, princesses," shouted Periwinkle, "we aren't far from Coral Castle. We just need to pass over Deepwater Drop. It's a bit choppy, but I think we'll be able to make it. We are the royal seahorses, after all. So if anyone can do it, we can!"

"Are you sure?" said Buttercup, thinking that the seahorses already looked very tired. "Perhaps we should find shelter and ride out the storm. It really doesn't matter if we miss the party."

"Oh," said Violet, looking disappointed. "But we've come all this way. It would be a shame to miss it."

"No need to worry," said Periwinkle. "I think this is just a little shower, not a full-blown glitter storm. Hold on to your hair clips, though – we could get shaken up a bit over the drop."

The princesses held on to their hair clips and each other as the sand fell away beneath them and they began to pass over the deep ocean trench. The water was so deep here that they couldn't see the bottom, just a steep wall of coral stretching down into the dark water.

The seahorses were swimming hard now, their small, delicate fins fanning

the water to push themselves against the
strong current. More and more glitter
whooshed past them and it was getting
difficult to see out of the carriage.

The fairy princesses noticed that the current was starting to pull the swirling glitter and the carriage downwards.

"Not much further now," said Rosa, pointing ahead of them. "I can see the other side of the trench."

The seahorses pushed as hard as they could through the swirling glitter and the first two had nearly made it on to the bank when the carriage jolted backwards. It was no use; the current was too strong for the four seahorses to swim against.

"Princesses," shouted Buttercup, "I've got an idea. The carriage is too heavy and we aren't going to make it. Throw your luggage out over the side. That might be just enough to get us safely on to the bank."

"Our bags!" exclaimed Violet. "What about our outfits? We'll have nothing to wear to the Glitter Ball."

"Don't worry about that," said Buttercup. "If we don't throw them out, the seahorses will be in serious trouble. We need to do it now!" she said, tossing her own sparkly yellow weekend bag over the side and into the deep ocean. The others did the same as quickly as they could.

The carriage rose slightly in the water

and the front seahorses were able to pull themselves forward towards the ledge. The princesses were so close they could almost reach out and touch the bank. But it was no use – the current was still too strong for the seahorses to pull the carriage with them.

"What do we do now?" shouted Violet to Buttercup over the roaring water. She could see the seahorses didn't have the strength to make another attempt and the current was getting stronger.

"Get out and swim!" shouted Buttercup. "Swim as hard as you can to the bank. The carriage will be lighter without us in it."

Violet, Rosa and Bluebell leapt out of their seats and swam as hard as they could to the bank. When they got there, the three fairy princesses took shelter beneath an empty scallop shell. Buttercup swam

to the front of the carriage to help guide
the seahorses on to the ledge.

"We will be all right, Princess," said
Periwinkle weakly. "The carriage is much
lighter now. Please go and join your
friends."

"I'm not going to leave you," said

Buttercup. Periwinkle was right, the carriage was much lighter, but they looked so tired now and she wasn't sure they would be able to make it through the swirling, glittering water.

Buttercup knew she had to do something. After seeing how bravely the seahorses had struggled to pull them through the storm, she desperately wanted to help them in return. She looked quickly about her to see if there was anything she could use to help. For a moment all she could see was swirling sand, until suddenly she caught sight of something glinting on the sea floor close to where the other princesses were sheltering. A jagged piece of broken oyster shell. *That might just do it*, she thought to herself, swimming over and grabbing the shell in her delicate hand and then swimming back to the seahorses.

"Buttercup," shouted Violet, "come back! The current is too strong."

"What is she doing?" said Rosa, clasping Violet's hand for comfort.

"She cares for the seahorses," said Bluebell, frightened for her friend but admiring her courage.

Buttercup swam towards the seahorses through the stinging glitter. She reached them quickly, as she was helped by the fast current pulling them under. She took hold of the seaweed reins and cut them free from the heavy carriage with one stroke of the sharp shell. Buttercup leapt on to Periwinkle's shiny back and urged him upwards with a gentle kick. The seahorses, seeing that they were no longer tied to the heavy carriage, swam hard and reached the bank in less than a minute.

Chapter 6

When Buttercup reached the bank with the four seahorses, the glitter storm had started to die down. She was met by three very worried fairy princesses, who came fluttering out from under the scallop shell.

"Buttercup! Thank goodness you're safe," said Violet, helping her down from the tired seahorse and wrapping her in a big hug. "What were you thinking?"

"I didn't have time to think," said
Buttercup, catching her breath. "I just
knew I couldn't leave the seahorses to
go down with that carriage."

"You were very brave indeed," said
Periwinkle, seeing Buttercup in a new
light. "I can't thank you enough. We owe
you our lives."

Buttercup blushed. She honestly didn't think she had done anything brave at all. She just knew that she had wanted to help the seahorses.

Rosa thought for a moment. "There are four seahorses and four of us," she said. "Periwinkle, do you think we could ride on your backs the rest of the way? If you're not too tired, of course."

"It would be an honour," said Periwinkle, bending his head so that Buttercup could climb on to his back again.

The four princesses mounted the seahorses and continued their journey to the castle. They travelled quietly now, relieved to have made it safely through the storm and looking forward to being able to relax at the party.

It was only when Buttercup glanced over at her friends that she realized they

were all still wearing their beach clothes.
What's more, the storm had played havoc
with their hair. Violet's was curlier than
ever, and Bluebell's normally stylish bob
was sticking up in different directions.
They certainly didn't look ready for a ball.

"Oh no!" said Buttercup, remembering
the bags they had thrown over the side.
"Our outfits. Great-aunt Melinda went

to such trouble to find us those dresses. I don't know what I'm going to tell her when I see her."

"I'm sure she will understand," said Rosa. "We really couldn't help it – we were about to be dragged down into Deepwater Drop by the glitter storm."

"At least we still have our hair clips," said Bluebell. "We would have been upset if we had lost those."

"One thing's for sure: we certainly can't go to the ball like this," said Violet, looking down at her crumpled sarong. "Perhaps we should just turn round and go home."

Buttercup listened but didn't say anything. She knew they had done the right thing, but she was so disappointed. She wrapped her arms more tightly around Periwinkle to make herself feel better. She knew that she must be imagining it, but she felt that Periwinkle could tell how she was feeling.

As the fashion fairy princesses drew closer to Coral Castle, they started to see other merpeople making their way to the ball. They had shimmering skin and fishes' tails that seemed to change colour as they moved. The merpeople either rode on the backs of seahorses or brightly coloured fish, or travelled in glittering carriages, just like the one they had left behind at Deepwater Drop. Unlike the fashion fairy princesses, they were all beautifully dressed.

The fairy princesses were admiring the merpeoples' sparkling outfits when they spotted King Neptune's Coral Castle in the turquoise water ahead of them. It was magnificent. It stood on the edge of the coral with the reef stretching out before it like a beautiful garden. The castle was also made of brightly coloured coral. It had four towers topped with beautiful sea anemones, waving in the gentle current like flags. The windows of the castle were framed with gleaming pearls, and bright shells decorated the walls. At the entrance stood two swordfish guarding the castle gate. Their shining silver scales looked like polished armour.

Buttercup gasped. "Isn't it beautiful!" she said, admiring the garden that was filled with exotic fish and colourful shells and crabs. "Can you imagine living somewhere like this?"

"It is beautiful," said Violet, smiling, "but I don't think I would want to risk another glitter storm."

"Buttercup," said Bluebell, pointing into
the crowd of merpeople pouring into the
castle's clamshell doors, "there's a mermaid

over there waving at you. Is that your Great-aunt Melinda?"

As she spoke, a plump mermaid with curly red hair and wearing a bright green dress swam excitedly towards them.

"Yoo-hoo, Buttercup!" she said, waving at her blushing niece. "You made it. I was so worried you would get stuck in that horrid glitter storm. Let me take a good look at you all."

Buttercup, Violet, Rosa and Bluebell climbed off the seahorses, who swam away before the fairy princesses could thank them. The princesses stood before Melinda as she peered at them over the sea-green spectacles perched on the end of her nose.

"Oh dear," she said, wrinkling her nose and causing her spectacles to slip, "I see that you need to dress for the ball.

Not to worry. You can change in my
carriage. I trust you picked up the
gowns?" She looked about them for their
bags.

Buttercup stared down at her feet as
she nervously dug them into the sandy
sea floor.

"We lost them," she mumbled, "in the glitter storm. We had to throw them out of the carriage with all our things."

"Oh no!" Melinda cried. "You poor fairies! Thank goodness you weren't hurt. Well, I suppose you'll just have to come as you are," she said, frowning at the fashion fairy princesses' messy hair and storm-battered clothes. "At least you have those beautiful hair clips. I'm sure it will be fine if we explain."

"Melinda!" said a booming voice behind them. "It most certainly will not be fine. There is no way that I will allow them to attend *my* ball dressed as they are. And there is no need to explain. My royal seahorses have told me everything."

The four fairy princesses and Great-aunt Melinda spun round to see an enormous golden carriage, drawn by six glittering

sea dragons. Sitting behind the sea dragons
on a mother-of-pearl throne was King
Neptune himself. He had a long, glittering
beard, and was wearing a crown made
from twisted coral and decorated with
enormous pearls. Swimming beside him
were the four royal seahorses.

· · • Chapter 7 • · ·

"Which one of you is Princess Buttercup?" boomed Neptune, staring down at the frightened fashion fairy princesses standing in front of him.

"I am," whispered Buttercup, lowering her eyes and flushing pink. She had never been so frightened in all her life.

"I'm sorry, I can't hear you. Please step towards my carriage so that I can take a better look at you," said Neptune.

Seeing that Buttercup was about to cry, one of the seahorses swam up beside her and gave her a gentle nudge with its long nose. Buttercup stepped forward, taking courage from the friendly push.

"I'm Buttercup," she said more bravely. "I'm so sorry to turn up at your ball dressed as we are. Great-aunt Melinda reserved us such beautiful dresses, but I am afraid we lost them in the storm and. . ."

Buttercup stopped speaking as Neptune swam down from his carriage and took a deep bow in front of the trembling fairy princess. As he came closer, Buttercup thought she could see a twinkle in the old merman's eye. Neptune then took Buttercup's tiny hand in his and shook it vigorously.

"It is a great honour for me to meet you, Princess Buttercup. My name is Neptune, king of the merpeople," said the wise king as he looked at the tiny, frightened fairy standing before him. *Could such a nervous little fairy really have shown so much courage in saving my royal seahorses?* he thought to himself.

"Please, do not worry about your

outfits. What you wear on the outside can be changed in an instant," said Neptune. "It is what is inside a fairy that lasts for ever. You may appear shy on the outside, Princess Buttercup, but inside you are one of the bravest and most courageous fairies I have ever had the honour of meeting."

Violet, Rosa and Bluebell gasped while Great-aunt Melinda looked on, amazed that her shy little niece could be singled out for bravery. Buttercup's cheeks turned a deep red as Neptune continued.

"After you arrived at the castle, the seahorses came to find me and told me all about what you did to save them. We merpeople prize courage above any other virtue. I would be grateful if you and your fashion fairy princess friends would do me the honour of accompanying me to the Glitter Ball as my extra-special guests."

Buttercup didn't know what to say. She really didn't think had ever done anything brave. In fact, most of the time she didn't feel brave at all! Before she could pluck up the courage to answer the wise king, Violet answered for her.

"We would be honoured to come, King Neptune," she said, "but as you mentioned before, we can't attend the ball dressed as we are."

Buttercup looked at her friend admiringly. Violet really did have the confidence to speak to anyone.

"Violet is right," said Buttercup, taking courage from her friend and nervously addressing the king. "I'm so sorry, King Neptune. Thank you for all those nice things you said about me. We would love to come to your ball as your special guests, but we don't have anything to wear, so I am afraid. . ."

"Buttercup!" said Neptune, with a booming belly laugh. "Weren't you listening to me? I told you that your outfits could be changed in an instant. It is what is *inside* a fairy that counts, and I can see that there is a brave heart inside you too, Violet."

Neptune smiled at the outspoken fairy princess and then placed his hands on the friends' shoulders. "Please," he said, waving towards the smiling seahorses. "The seahorses will take you to my royal weaver fish. They will make you some beautiful brand-new outfits. Melinda and I will go on to the ball and make sure nothing starts until my guests of honour arrive." Neptune linked arms with a speechless Great-aunt Melinda and helped her into the carriage.

"Don't worry, Melinda, I'll explain everything on the way." He looked over his shoulder and winked at the four fashion fairy princesses.

"See you later, princesses. The royal weaver fish will take good care of you," he said as his golden carriage pulled away, leaving them in a cloud of tiny bubbles.

Violet, Rosa, Buttercup and Bluebell looked at one another and laughed. It was turning out to be a day full of surprises.

Chapter 8

The four fashion fairy princesses followed
the seahorses into a pretty shop built
into the side of a pearly shell. The shop
was much bigger on the inside than it
looked from the outside. The walls were
lined with hundreds of rolls of beautiful
fabric in every colour imaginable. The
fairies looked around as they waited for
the seahorses to explain the situation to a

shoal of silver, needle-shaped weaver fish that greeted them as they came in.

"This fabric isn't like anything I've ever seen before," said Bluebell, fingering some bright blue netting. "What is it made of?"

"That netting is made of a type of seaweed called kelp," said Rosa, "and the weaver fish dye it using ink from rainbow squid that comes in any colour you can think of."

"It's wonderfully soft," Bluebell said.

"I'm so glad you like it," remarked one of the tiny, needle-shaped fish as it swam towards the fairies. "We will certainly use some in the gown we create for you. May we begin?"

"Yes, please!" said Buttercup. "We really don't want to keep everyone waiting."

No sooner had she spoken than the four princesses were each set upon by a cloud of smiling weaver fish. Some took measurements, working in pairs to hold up the tape measures; some noted things down; and others flitted quickly between the shelves of glittering fabric.

"Ha ha ha, that tickles!" giggled Violet, as an apologetic weaver fish swam out from under her arm carrying a tape measure.

The fairy princesses were then shown small pieces of fabric, called swatches, so that they could choose which colour they would like their gowns to be. Rosa chose a soft pink, Violet a deep purple, Buttercup a bright yellow, and Bluebell, the blue netting she had seen when she came in.

Now they had decided on their fabrics, the little fish really got to work. Each of the fairy princesses was covered from the neck down in a cloud of tiny glittering bubbles made by the fast-working fish. Another group set to work on the princesses' hair, combing out the tangles with their needle-shaped noses.

"Well, this the first time fish have made us dresses," said Rosa, smiling.

"I can't believe how quickly they're working," said Buttercup. "King Neptune was right when he said it would take only an instant."

At that moment, the clouds of tiny bubbles covering them vanished. The fish swam to the other side of the shop to let the princesses look at their new gowns in the full-length mirrors.

"That's incredible," said Rosa, staring at their reflections. "They're almost the same as the dresses we lost in Deepwater Drop."

"Except they are even more beautiful," said Buttercup, gently touching the golden pearls on her bodice.

"The fishtail skirts look even more real!" said Violet, giving a little twirl and swishing her tail. "And they go perfectly with our seahorse hair clips."

"How could you know what our dresses looked like?" Buttercup asked the smiling weaver fish.

"We were the ones who designed them and sent them over to Serena Seaspray," one of the fish replied. "We have been designing all her gowns for years."

The princesses took one last look in the mirror, adjusted their clips and climbed back on to the seahorses.

"Thank you so much!" said Buttercup.

"It was our pleasure," said another fish. "Please visit us again the next time you come to Glitter Ocean."

Buttercup assured them that they would, and all four fairy princesses waved goodbye as the seahorses whisked them off to the Glitter Ball.

As the fairies arrived at Coral Castle, they could see all the merpeople gathered outside the great doors, waving at them. The four seahorses swam through the welcoming crowd and up to the front, where Neptune and Great-aunt Melinda were standing. King Neptune smiled and beckoned Buttercup and the princesses to come closer.

Violet nudged Buttercup to go first, but Buttercup stood glued to the spot.

"Please, Violet," said Buttercup, looking

nervously at the crowd of waving merpeople,
"I can't stand in front of everyone alone.
Tell me you'll come with me."

"Of course I will," she said, linking arms with her friend. "We fashion fairy princesses stick together!"

Once they were in front of King Neptune and Great-aunt Melinda, Neptune called the crowd of well-dressed merpeople to be quiet and then told them all about what Buttercup had done to save the seahorses.

"And that is why I have asked the fashion fairy princesses to be my extra-special guests at this year's Glitter Ball. In recognition for their bravery and as a reminder of their adventures in Glitter Ocean, I would like to present them with the Order of the Ocean, the highest honour that can be awarded to any fairy visiting our underwater kingdom."

Buttercup, Rosa, Bluebell and Violet stepped forward in turn as King Neptune presented each of them with a beautiful golden seahorse pendant and fastened it around their necks. The merpeople burst into applause.

"And now," said Neptune, hushing the crowd yet again, "let the Glitter Ball begin!"

Neptune led the four fashion fairy princesses into the castle and through to the Great Hall, which had been decorated with beautiful glittering shells. Seaweed in a rainbow of colours hung from the ceiling's pearl chandeliers like streamers and paper chains. Tables, piled high with delicious-looking cupcakes, chocolate sea-foam fountains, and all different kinds of sweet sea treats, stood against the walls to make way for an enormous dance floor in the centre of the room.

The fairy princesses gasped when they saw the beautiful room. There was so much to see, they didn't know which way

to go first. Should they run to the tables and taste the glittering cupcakes or hit the dance floor? Their minds were soon made up when a shoal of party fish swam on to the stage at the front of the room and started playing a catchy tune on instruments made of polished driftwood.

"Look, Buttercup!" said Bluebell, doing a twirl right in the centre of the dance floor. "There's Periwinkle with the rest of the seahorses. Do you think they would like to dance?"

"I'll go and see," said Buttercup, swimming off quickly towards them.

In a moment she was back, and the fashion fairy princesses and the seahorses danced together in the Great Hall until they were ready to drop. Even Great-aunt Melinda came over to join them. She had great fun teaching the princesses a few

dance moves she'd learned when she was
a young mermaid.

"Let's get something to drink," said

Buttercup. "All this salt water is making me thirsty."

The fairy princesses left the dance floor and swam over to a table with a punchbowl made out of a spiral sea-snail shell.

"I don't know when I last had so much fun," said Buttercup, taking a sip of the delicious sea-fruit cocktail.

"And it turns out that you're braver than you think," said Violet, giving her friend a little wink.

"I don't know about that," said Buttercup, smiling, "but I would definitely come to Glitter Ocean again, though I might check the weather first!"

The four fashion fairy princesses laughed and headed back to the dance floor arm in arm.

Later, when the princesses were very tired and tucked up in their seashell beds

at Great-aunt Melinda's house, the four
friends promised each other that they
would have another underwater adventure
in Glitter Ocean soon.

If you enjoyed this

Fashion Fairy Princess

book then why not visit our
magical new website!

- Explore the enchanted world of the fashion fairy princesses
- Find out which fairy princess you are
- Download sparkly screensavers
- Make your own tiara
- Colour in your own picture frame and much more!

fashionfairyprincess.com

Journey deeper into the world of
the fashion fairy princesses with more
exciting adventures!

Use the stickers from these activity books to give Buttercup a magical makeover on the following page.

And coming soon...